In a Small Kingdom

For Lynn Caponera and Dona Ann McAdams,
who crossed my path with Doug Salati's
—T. deP.

For my parents, Carol and Aldo
—D. S.

SIMON & SCHUSTER
BOOKS FOR YOUNG READERS
An imprint of Simon & Schuster Children's
Publishing Division • 1230 Avenue of the Americas,
New York, New York 10020 • Text copyright © 2018 by Tomie
dePaola • Illustrations copyright © 2018 by Douglas Steele Salati • All
rights reserved, including the right of reproduction in whole or in part in
any form. • SIMON & SCHUSTER BOOKS FOR YOUNG READERS is a
trademark of Simon & Schuster, Inc. • For information about special discounts
for bulk purchases, please contact Simon & Schuster Special Sales at 1-866-
506-1949 or business@simonandschuster.com. • The Simon & Schuster Speakers
Bureau can bring authors to your live event. For more information or to book an
event, contact the Simon & Schuster Speakers Bureau at 1-866-248-3049 or visit our
website at www.simonspeakers.com. • Book design by Laurent Linn • The text for this
book was set in Cantoria MT Std. • The illustrations for this book were rendered in
graphite and charcoal pencil and colored digitally. • Manufactured in China • 0118 SCP
• First Edition • 10 9 8 7 6 5 4 3 2 1 • Library of Congress Cataloging-in-Publication
Data • Names: DePaola, Tomie, 1934– author. | Salati, Doug, illustrator. • Title: In
a small kingdom / by Caldecott honor and Newbery honor winner Tomie dePaola
; illustrated by Doug Salati. • Description: First edition. | New York : Simon &
Schuster Books for Young Readers, [2018] | Summary: "This folkloric picture book
tells the story of a magical robe that goes missing, and the kingdom that hangs
in the balance"— Provided by publisher. • Identifiers: LCCN 2016032790
| ISBN 9781481498005 (hardcover) | ISBN 9781481498012 (eBook) •
Subjects: | CYAC: Kings, queens, rulers, etc.—Fiction. | Clothing
and dress—Fiction. • Classification: LCC PZ7.D439 In 2018
| DDC [E]—dc23 LC record available at https://
lccn.loc.gov/2016032790

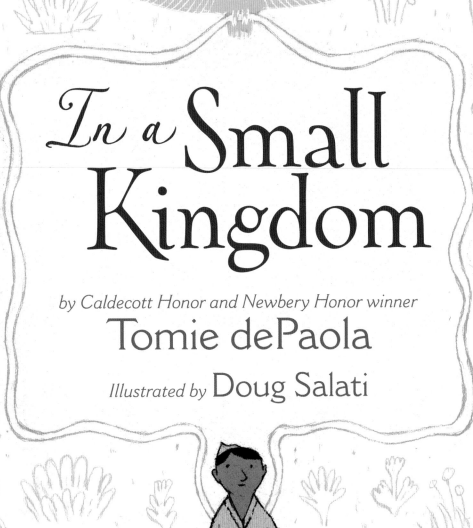

In a Small Kingdom

by Caldecott Honor and Newbery Honor winner
Tomie dePaola

Illustrated by Doug Salati

SIMON & SCHUSTER BOOKS FOR YOUNG READERS

New York   London   Toronto   Sydney   New Delhi

In a small kingdom along an ancient road, a bell rang out in the middle of the night. Townspeople and travelers from all across the kingdom rushed to the palace.

As the balcony doors opened, the chief counselor stepped forward and announced, "The old king is dead."

A cry rose up, for the old king, being fair and just, was much loved.

The small kingdom had flourished under his long rule as a place of safety for caravans. It was said that the king had possessed secret powers against bandits and thieves that rested in a magnificent Imperial Robe, which few had ever seen.

But now that the old king was dead . . . what would the future bring?

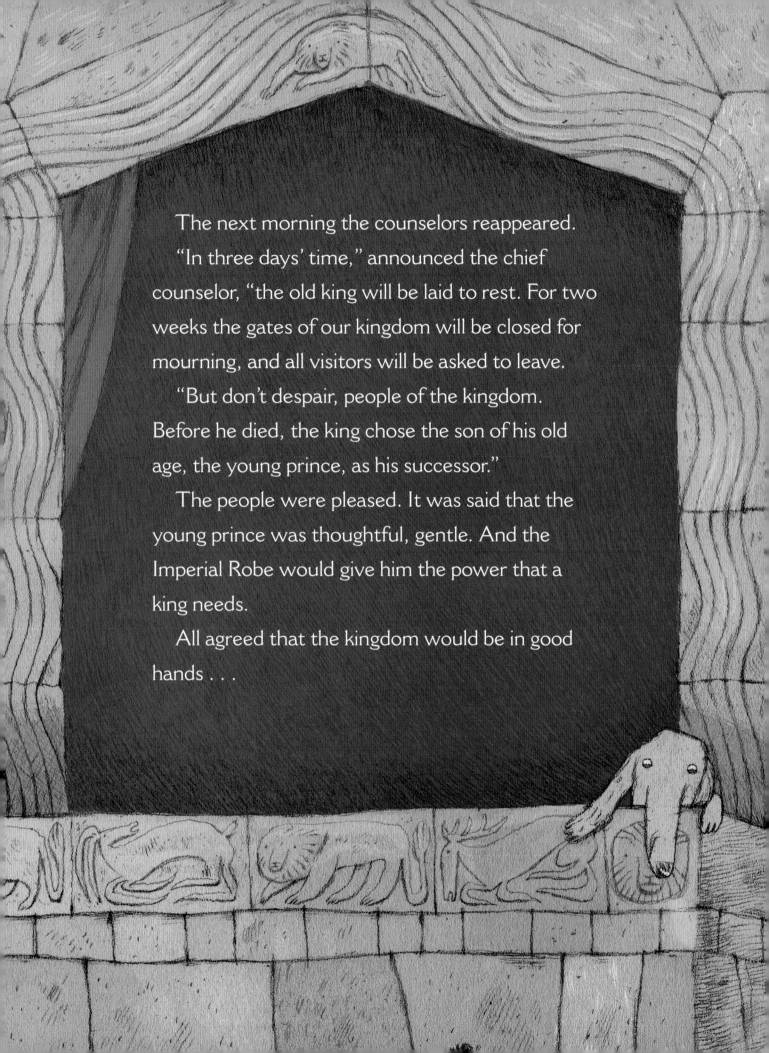

The next morning the counselors reappeared.

"In three days' time," announced the chief counselor, "the old king will be laid to rest. For two weeks the gates of our kingdom will be closed for mourning, and all visitors will be asked to leave.

"But don't despair, people of the kingdom. Before he died, the king chose the son of his old age, the young prince, as his successor."

The people were pleased. It was said that the young prince was thoughtful, gentle. And the Imperial Robe would give him the power that a king needs.

All agreed that the kingdom would be in good hands . . .

. . . except for one person. The young prince's older half brother seethed with jealousy. "The old king was my father too," he said to himself. "How dare he choose my half brother to be king?"

In an instant the angry half brother knew what he would do. *Without the Robe, the young prince cannot rule,* he thought. *He is too young, too weak. But I am not.*

That very night the half brother broke into the
wardrobe where the Imperial Robe was locked away
and took it to the top of a high tower.

He slashed it to bits, scattering the torn pieces.
Now he would wait.

The time of mourning came to an end, and the young prince was led to the wardrobe.

"The Imperial Robe is so powerful, you will only wear it in the inner rooms of the palace," the chief counselor told the prince. "It is time to see this remarkable garment."

You can imagine the horror everyone felt when they saw that the Robe was gone!

The poor prince fled in despair and locked himself away.
Without the Robe, he could not be king!

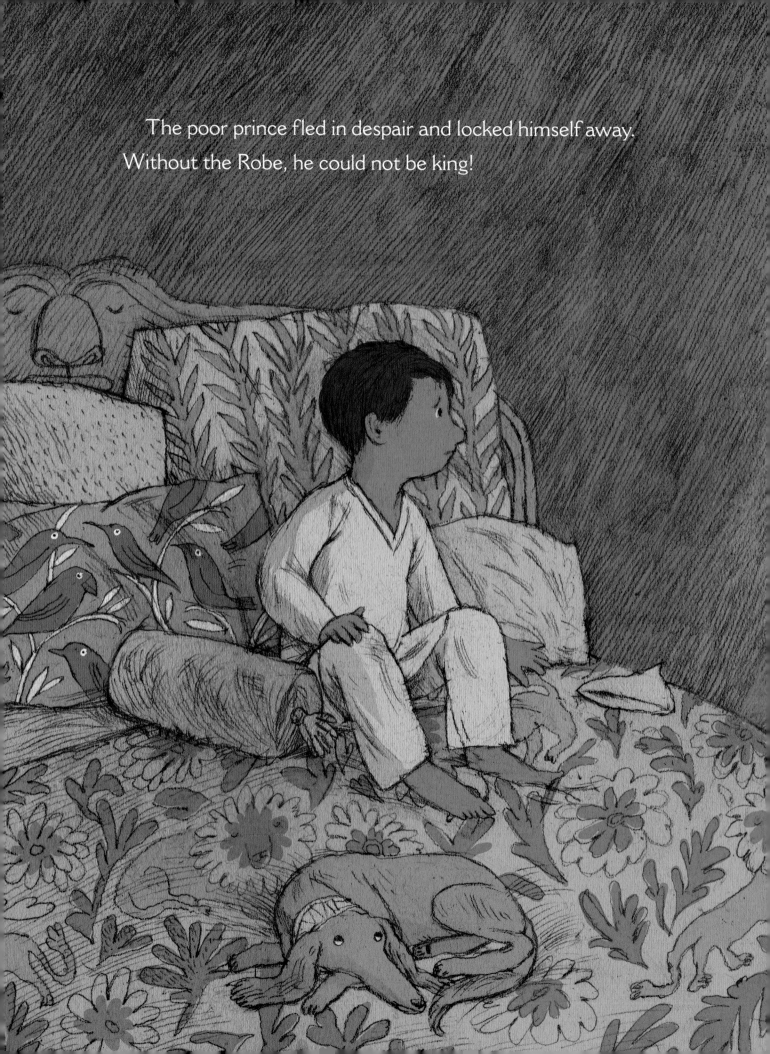

Without a ruler, the small kingdom was in danger. Anyone could attack and take over. So the gates were kept shut. The inns and guesthouses stayed empty. But without visitors, the kingdom would soon be penniless.

The townspeople were desolate. No one knew what to do.

They needed the Robe. Where was it?

Only the half brother knew. With the Robe destroyed, the
kingdom would soon become desperate, and he would step in
to take his place as ruler. He prepared to put his plan into action.

Around this same time, in a humble part of the kingdom, some children were playing by the river.

"Look what I found," called a girl as the other children crowded around. "It's the most beautiful cloth I have ever seen. And there are more pieces over here—and more over there."

"Let's bring them to Amah. She is so wise. She'll know what they are," said a boy.

So they did.

"Why, these are fragments of the Imperial Robe," Amah said. "When I was a young seamstress at court, I once repaired the sleeve."

As Amah gently held the glimmering pieces, she knew what had to be done.

"Children, go back to the river," Amah said. "Look everywhere for other fragments."

Together the children found more—and more—and more.

Amah gathered those who could sew.

They sewed and sewed, but still fragments were missing.

"Tell everyone to bring a piece of fabric that is precious to them," said Amah. "If they give lovingly, the Robe can be completed."

And the people did.

"Here is a small piece from my wedding veil," an old woman said.

"This is a bit of the blanket we used to protect our child when she was very ill," said a mother and father. "She is grown now."

"My grandfather gave me this scarf to keep the sun off my neck," said a boy.

"This is from the coat of the beautiful doll my aunt brought me from the caravan," said a young girl.

Over and over, people brought pieces of precious things from their lives.

And Amah and the people sewed into the Robe every treasured fragment that could be found.

When the Robe was finished, it did not look the same
as before, but a new and extraordinary pattern appeared.
The people took the Robe to the palace.
"It is for our new king," the people said.

The counselors brought the Robe to the forlorn young prince and told him what had been done.

"The people found fragments of the Imperial Robe and sewed them together with fragments from their own lives," said the chief counselor. "They did it out of love for you and for the kingdom."

"Then I shall wear it," said the prince. "But I will be robed in public. All shall see the new mystical Robe."

The counselors were amazed at the newfound strength of the young prince.

The half brother witnessed this from the shadows.

"The Robe has been found," he said to himself. "I must leave the kingdom before the Robe destroys me."

And off into the night he fled, and was never seen or heard from again.

The very next day, for the first time, the people
saw their new king in the Imperial Robe.
It was a thing of mystery, power, and beauty.

"My people," the young king declared, "this Robe that I wear not only has the power but also your love. . . .

"Just as you have the love of your new king."